GIRLS ROCK!
Contents

KT-467-762

Jess   *Sophie*

CHAPTER 1

High Score, Low Score

Sophie and Jess arrive at the local minigolf course. They wave goodbye to Jess's mum, who leaves them to play a game while she goes to the shops.

Sophie "I love minigolf."

Jess "First time for me."

Sophie (laughing) "Don't worry. I'll give you tips—and I'll try not to win by too much."

The girls pay the entry fee and choose their golf balls.

Sophie "Green for me. It's my lucky colour."

Jess "I'll take blue. Does this match my eyes?"

Sophie "Well, it's bigger than your eyes, and it doesn't have any eyelashes. No, it doesn't really match your eyes."

The woman gives the girls scorecards, pencils and golf clubs.

Sophie "I'll show you how to hold the club. Put your feet like this ... and hold your hands like this."

Jess "Golf seems complicated."

Sophie "Not really. Just follow me."

Jess "How many holes are there?"

Sophie "Eighteen."

The first hole is a long, straight cement path with a little hole at the end.

Jess "So I hit the ball in that hole? Shouldn't be too hard."

Sophie (laughing) "It looks easy. You go first."

Jess takes the first shot. The ball
flies off the path and out of bounds.

Jess "Now what?"

Sophie "Stick the ball on the white
line near where it went out. Whack
it again."

Jess takes six more strokes to get the ball in the hole.

Jess "Pretty good for my first time."
Sophie (laughing) "If you say so."

Sophie hits the ball. It rolls down the centre of the path right into the cup. *Clink!* Jess keeps score:
Jess, 7. Sophie, 1.

Jess "Wow! My score is so much higher than yours. I'm winning."

Sophie "I forgot to tell you. In golf, low score wins. You're losing."

Jess "Losing? I don't think so. This game's just getting started."

CHAPTER 2

The Volcano

The girls soon arrive at Hole 4, which is a curved path with a small, smooth hill at the far end. The hole is in the middle of the hill.

Jess "What's that?"

Sophie "The Volcano. You have to hit your ball up the little hill, into the cup."

As Jess gets ready to swing, a little bird lands on the ground near where she is standing.

Jess "What a cute bird."
Sophie "Don't lose focus."

Jess takes five strokes to land her ball in the cup at the top of the Volcano. The little bird begins to sing.

Jess "Hi, little birdie. Are you here to cheer me on?"

Sophie "That bird is here to cheer you up—when you lose."

Jess (smiling) "We'll see who loses. Your turn, Sophie."

Sophie prepares to take her shot. Jess kneels down by the bird.

Sophie "You're not actually talking to that bird, are you?"

Jess "The birdie says you are not holding your hands the right way."

Sophie "I'd like to see how that bird would hold a golf club!"

Sophie whacks the ball extra hard and it flies out of bounds. She places it back in bounds and takes shot after shot until Jess interrupts.

Jess "Sophie, stop. Your turn's over."

Sophie "What are you talking about?"

Jess "You're not allowed to take more than seven shots for each hole."

Sophie "How do you know that?"

Jess "I'd say a little birdie told me, but it's written in the rules. On the scorecard. Let's move on."

Jess leads a grumbling Sophie to the next hole.

CHAPTER 3

Scary Skeleton

The girls play through more holes to arrive at Hole 13, which is a skeleton head with an open mouth.

Jess "Let me guess. We hit the ball in his mouth?"

Sophie "Yeah. Up the little hill painted pink like a tongue."

Jess "Doesn't look so hard."

Sophie "It's the uphill part that's hard. Remember the Volcano?"

Jess "I think you're the one who had the problem at the Volcano."

Sophie "I don't care. I'm still winning."

Jess "I'm about to change that."

Jess prepares her first shot. The bird sticks by her feet.

Jess "Soph, meet my new lucky charm."

Jess whacks the ball. It rolls up the hill, through the skeleton's mouth, and out the other side. Surprised, the girls run to the other side to see where the ball stops. Jess jumps up and down.

Jess "My first hole in one! That is so cool."

Sophie "Beginner's luck."

Jess "No way. I'm a natural. Your turn."

Sophie taps the ball. It goes slowly up the hill and into the skeleton's mouth. But the ball doesn't have enough power to make it all the way. It rolls up to the skeleton's mouth, stops for a split second and then rolls back down.

Jess (laughing) "The skeleton spat out your ball. Yuck! Skeleton spit."

Sophie takes another five shots to land her ball in the cup.

Sophie "That bird's getting on my nerves."

Jess pays no attention as she keeps score. The bird sits on her shoulder.

Jess "Guess who's winning? Me!"

Sophie (muttering) "I wish my cat Puffles could be here. He'd love a little snack."

Jess "Did you just say something?"

Sophie "I said, I think I have the sniffles, and I may have hurt my back."

Jess "That's too bad. Come on."

CHAPTER 4

Wicky Wacky Windmill

The girls soon get to Hole 17. It's a little windmill, with big blades that turn slowly. Two little garden gnomes guard the doorway to the windmill.

Jess "How does this work?"
Sophie "Watch the blades turn and you'll see."

The girls' heads move in a little circle as they watch the blades turn.

Sophie "See the little tunnel where the front door should be? You have to hit the ball through the doorway."

Jess "Between the blades?"

Sophie "Brilliant, Einstein."

Sophie notices that, instead of one bird hanging around Jess, there are now two.

Sophie "Why are those birds hanging around you?"

Jess tries not to laugh.

Jess "Animals like me. What can I say?"

Sophie "Whatever. Take your shot."

Jess swings her club backwards, but when she swings forwards, she misses the ball entirely.

Sophie (laughing) "Great air shot!
A few more like that and I'm sure
to win."

The girls play through the windmill.
In the end, each takes four strokes
to put the ball in the hole. Sophie
now sees a third bird hanging around
Jess—and she notices that Jess
keeps her hand in her pocket.

Sophie "What's in your pocket?"

Jess (blushing) "Nothing. Come on. Last hole. I mean, your last chance before I win."

Sophie "Wait a minute."

Jess runs ahead.

CHAPTER 5

The Raging River

The girls come to Hole 18, the last hole.

Sophie "You've got something in your pocket. What is it?"

Jess "I have no idea what you're talking about. Hey, look at this!"

Hole 18 is a cement mountain cut in half. In the middle there's a gap, like a canyon, of about one metre. At the bottom of the canyon, there's a bubbling brook.

Jess "You have to hit the ball uphill on this side."

Sophie "And you have to hit it hard enough to get it across the canyon."

Jess "If you don't, it'll fall in the water."

Sophie "But if you get it across the canyon, then it'll roll right into the hole."

Jess "That's an automatic hole in one! I love this game!"

Sophie "Your turn."

Jess hits the ball hard. It zooms up the hill and falls off the edge, into the water. While trying to pick up her ball, Jess slips on a wet rock and falls.

Jess "Sophie, help me."

As Sophie walks over to help, she notices about ten birds near where Jess is sitting.

Sophie "I'm not helping you up until you tell me something."

Jess "What?"

Sophie (yelling) "WHAT IS IT WITH ALL THE BIRDS? What's that white stuff you're sitting in?"

Laughing, Jess pulls her pocket inside out to show Sophie what she has been hiding.

Sophie "Popcorn!"

Jess "I grabbed some for a snack just before we left. It turns out that birds love this stuff!"

Sophie "That's how you got that bird to follow us around?"

Jess "Yeah. Cool, huh?"

Sophie "So she's not your magic lucky charm!"

Jess "Just a hungry bird."

Sophie (laughing) "Well, that makes me hungry. Let's finish this game and go get a real snack."

Jess "Yeah. This popcorn's for the birds."

Jess

GIRLS ROCK!
Minigolf Lingo

Sophie

back nine The last nine holes (holes 10–18) on an 18-hole golf course.

birdie A fluffy friend who might secretly coach you. It's also when you get your ball in the cup taking one less hit, or stroke, than par. Birdies are good things in golf!

cup The hole—where you want your ball to go.

front nine The first nine holes (holes 1–9) on an 18-hole golf course.

par The number of strokes it *should* take you to put your ball in the hole.

whiff To swing and miss the ball entirely ("you whiffed it!"). Also called an air shot.

GIRLS ROCK!
Minigolf Must-dos

☆ Always wear cool sunglasses and
   sunscreen if you play minigolf
   outdoors.

☆ Bring your lucky charm, if you've got
   one. Might help you get a hole in one!

☆ Bring your camera with you to the
   game. If you get a hole in one, get
   someone to take your photo so
   you can show your mum and dad
   (maybe you'll get on the telly, too).

☆ Never throw your club at anybody or
   anything because you are not playing
   very well (even if you're really mad).

☆ Make sure that you get a golf club
   that is the right height for you.

☆ Always keep some popcorn in your pocket and a bottle of water—in case you get hungry or thirsty on the course.

☆ Scope out the hole to figure out the best way to get your ball in the hole with the fewest number of strokes—then just hit the ball and have fun.

☆ Get a job at the minigolf course on the weekends so you can practise for free.

☆ Always have a nice snack after you play golf. Ice-cream is really good after a tough session of minigolf on a hot summer day.

Minigolf Instant Info

- Miniature golf is a game modelled after the real sport of golf.

- Miniature golf has many names including: Minigolf, Crazy Golf, Goofy Golf, Midget Golf, Wacky Golf, Pee Wee Golf and Rinky Dinky Golf.

- A perfect score on a course with 18 holes is … 18! That's a hole in one on every hole.

- The best way to improve your golf game (like any sport) is to study and practise, practise, practise.

- The width of the cup (the hole) in minigolf should be from 10 to 12 centimetres.

- A minigolf ball should be from 37 to 43 millimetres wide.

- Show respect to other players by following the rules—that includes turning off your mobile phone while you play!

- The first miniature golf course was The Ladies' Putting Club, built in St. Andrews, Scotland, in 1867. At that time, it was not acceptable for women to swing their arms above their shoulders in public, so this private space was created for women to play golf.

- The world record for minigolf is a score of 18 on an 18-hole course (that's a hole in one for each hole) for four games played in a row!

- In the 1920s, a lot of people played minigolf on the tops of tall buildings in New York City.

GIRLS ROCK!
Think Tank

1 What is par for a hole?

2 What are at least three other names for minigolf?

3 What keeps your eyes protected when you play minigolf in the summer?

4 What's a perfect score on a course with 18 holes?

5 What is the best way to improve your minigolf score?

6 What's the best snack to have during a minigolf game?

7 What happens if you whiff the ball?

8 What's the hardest hole to play in minigolf?

Answers

1 Par is the number of shots it *should* take to get your ball in the hole.

2 You can call minigolf by any of these names: Goofy Golf, Crazy Golf, Midget Golf, Pee Wee Golf, Wacky Golf and Rinky Dinky Golf.

3 A really cool pair of sunglasses or a hat with a visor will protect your eyes while you are playing minigolf outdoors.

4 A perfect score on a course with 18 holes is 18 (a hole in one on every hole).

5 The best way to improve your minigolf score is study and practise. So practise, practise!

6 The best snack to munch on during a minigolf game is anything you want to eat that isn't too messy (or popcorn in your pocket, if you want to attract some feathery fans).

7 If you whiff the ball, it means that you tried to hit the ball and you completely missed it (kind of embarrassing).

8 The hardest hole to play is the one where you cannot land your ball in the cup! So that could be any hole.

How did you score?

- If you got all 8 answers correct, start training for an international minigolf competition. You might win some serious money!

- If you got 6 answers correct, get a job at the local minigolf course at the weekends to practise your shots.

- If you got fewer than 4 answers correct, forget about golf and learn to play the violin!

Hey Girls!

I hope you had fun reading this story. You know what I love most about reading? I can open a book and read a fantastic story about funny people or cool animals without even moving. And I can read wherever I want—in my room, in the library, in the park— anywhere. (When I was little, I tried to read in the car, but it made me feel sick. If that happens to you, ask your mum or dad about using some headphones to listen to books recorded on CDs.)

Here are some ideas about how you can make "Minigolf Face-off" even more fun. At school, you and your friends can be actors and put on this story as a play. To bring the story to life, you can use props. What will help? A golf club? A golf ball? A fake bird? Some popcorn?

Who will be Sophie? Who will be Jess? Who will be the narrator? (That's the person who reads the parts between when Sophie or Jess says something.) Maybe a talent scout will visit your class and you'll be invited to Hollywood for a movie audition. No matter what happens, you'll have fun!

You know what my dad used to tell me? Readers are leaders. So keep reading!

And, always remember—Boys may think they rule, but Girls Rock!

Holly Smith Dinbergs

Holly

When We Were Kids

Jacqueline

Holly talked to Jacqueline, another *Girls Rock!* author.

Jacqueline "Do you like golf?"

Holly "I think the idea of golf is fun, but … um … the truth is …"

Jacqueline "What? What's the truth?"

Holly "I'm terrible at golf!"

Jacqueline "Can't you hit the ball? It's pretty easy to hit a golf ball."

Holly "Yeah, I can hit the ball. That's not the problem."

Jacqueline "So what's the problem?"

Holly "I just keep hitting and hitting the ball. I never manage to get it in the hole."

Jacqueline "So you won't be entering any golf competitions?"

Holly "Only if highest score wins!"

GIRLS ROCK!
What a Laugh!

Q Why did the golfer take an extra pair of trousers with her?

A She was afraid she might get a hole in one!

GIRLS ROCK!

Read about the fun
that girls have in these
GIRLS ROCK! titles:

Birthday Party Blues
Pony Club

Doubles Trouble
Football Crazy

Dance Fever
Minigolf Face-off

Trapeze Dreams
Two at the Zoo

... and 20 more great
titles to choose from!

GIRLS ROCK! books are
available from most booksellers.
For mail order information please
call Rising Stars on 0871 47 23 010
or visit www.risingstars-uk.com

44